Accolad(

For *Enduring Spirit*:

"Pagan's writing is a reckoning. Filled to the brim with fierce, bold, and sharp women. Her newest collection, *Enduring Spirit,* asks the hard questions of today's hard world. From a woman seeking empathy from her government but receiving none, to a young girl saved from abuse by a creature of folklore, these stories cross genres with ease and leave the reader wanting more. Pagan weaves discomfort into her pages with a sometimes brutal, sometimes tender gut-punch that leaves the reader breathless."

-Holly Lyn Walrath, Author of *Glimmerglass Girl*

"*Enduring Spirit* is a tribute to survival. We meet Pagan's protagonists, young and old, at their most vulnerable moments. She explores the dreadful, unflinchingly, yet navigates her characters' intimate defenses and small victories with subtlety and tenderness. For Pagan's characters, endurance is a state of mind. They find their safe places and guardian spirits in externalized fairy tale worlds, and in internal manifestations of hope. They have to tell themselves a story if they are to get to the other side. In these stories, we walk with them—listening, watching, and hoping."

-Maya Kanwal, Award-winning Writer

"From a shape-shifting ghost rabbit to a political activist who has reached the end of her tether, Pagan has an unflinching way of evoking enormous emotion with few words. This collection boasts some stories with strong speculative elements, and others that take a close gaze at our all-to-human condition. *Enduring Spirit* is a collection to not only marvel at, but ponder upon."

-Eden Royce, Speculative Literature Foundation's Diverse Worlds Grant Winner

ENDURING SPIRIT

Stories

PATRICIA FLAHERTY PAGAN

CONTENTS

"Puca Dawns" reprinted from *Tides of Impossibility,* Published by Houston Writers Guild, 2015.

"The Stain of Caterpillars" created from "Gypsy Moth Summer," published in *Dual Coast Magazine*, 2017.

"Blood-red Geraniums" reprinted from *Waves of Suspense,* Houston Writers Guild, 2015.

"Angels of Pont-Saint Esprit" reprinted from *Cleaver Magazine*, 2015.

"Kit-Cat Clock" Reprinted from *Approaching Footsteps*, Spider Road Press, 2016.

"The meaning of fiction is not abstract meaning
but experienced meaning."
-Flannery O'Connor

INTRODUCTION

Stories are my lantern in the storm. They're my balm, my trial, my open hand, and my raised fist. Two thousand seventeen was a year of rising Texas floods, howling winds, and political tempests. As I curated my stories, I felt, acutely, the "tension—between private work and public duty, between art and life itself" as described so well in Joe Fassler's powerful essay, "Why Write Fiction in 2017?" Indeed, for a writer, reader, mother, and activist, the larger question is, why write when the culture I love is under threat?

My response to this question: Because fiction forges connection. Allies clasp hands on the page. Furthermore, I am braver in my fiction than I am in real life. So the stories in this collection, written in varied genres, speak to truths in my life and the lives of my loved ones and mentors. These are tales of survival, the interplay of danger, mystery, loyalty, identity, magic, and karma.

Writing time is precious. As I am blessed with family and teaching, my time with my stories feels hard-won. However, the challenge is worth it. As the narratives flow, I midwife the characters demanding to be born and offer them to you, dear reader. The survivors and fantastical visitors in these pages emerged from my heart. I hope they will work their way into yours.

Patricia Flaherty Pagan

April 2018

Púca Dawns

"Ghost playground? Ha-ha. Dumb boys. Who would haunt dead grass?" the pale, brown-haired girl with bruised legs beneath a clean gingham dress asked the gnarled tree on the edge of the overgrown lot.

Maeve thought fear was like electricity; it buzzed around behind things, but you usually couldn't see it. Maeve wouldn't step on a crack, in case she broke her mama's back. She wouldn't play with Ouija boards. She wouldn't eat grasshopper pie, just in case, but only one man made her feel hold-your-breath scared. So she went to the abandoned playground that Tuesday as afternoon shadows began to reach for the sun. It didn't look scary. It looked like a good place to fall down.

Walking across the brown grass, Maeve hummed the Scooby Doo theme song. Then she climbed on top of a boulder perched atop a small hill and rocked back and forth on her heels. "One . . . two . . . three."

Curious, a hazel beast serpentined his way through the undergrowth inching closer, ever closer, to surprise her. Yet she faced away from him, unmoved.

"Richard? Jay? I know one of you is there. You double-dared the entire class to come here at night. Now push me off. I won't tell."

The púca reared his tall, ram-like horns upwards and revealed his furry face. He pulled from the fading day's heat a booming voice. "Richard I'm not, but push you I shall!" His hoof gently tapped her shoulder blade. Then the púca snarled with glee as the little girl tumbled off the large rock and down the small hill to the dirt below. Thud.

Rising slowly, the girl checked her knees for new scratches and felt along the hem of her dress for rips. She found several.

"I really did fall and rip my dress. I did. Thanks, Jay. Don't tell any—"

Her blue eyes rose to meet his yellow ones and the relief deserted her voice. The púca rubbed one hoof across his bearded chin and smiled.

Maeve gaped at him.

"The pleasure's all mine, tumbling girl."

She ran. Dazed, the girl raced home, refused supper, and apologized to her mother for falling, ripping her dress, and bruising her legs.

"It wasn't real," Maeve whispered as she wrapped herself in a cocoon of purple cotton sheets that night. Then she surrendered to a fitful sleep marked by dreams of black horses with glowing eyes.

One week later, he sensed her on his land and sang her to him with a lullaby from the age before language. "You haven't brought me a carrot, Maeve."

The girl started, dropping her small, brown paper bag. "Who's there?" she gasped.

From behind a sagging and diseased oak, a gray rabbit the size of a German shepherd dog emerged. Maeve said nothing but stared at the patches of dirty, matted fur on his back and his long ears lined with peachy sheen. Her hands trembled. His earthy, foul scent enveloped her. Fascinated, Maeve smelled burnt cake and fresh mud mixed with her grandmother's allspice.

"The swings have long since fallen down." The rabbit-spirit waved a paw at the lone metal pole which remained, listing from years of January snows. "Who are Richard and Jay, and why do you cross my fields?"

Maeve frowned. She braided and unbraided one of her pigtails. "Richard's in my class. He picks his nose. Jay is his dumb friend. But rabbits don't talk. Except in movies."

Two prominent buckteeth shone as the púca flashed a mad

grin. "So, what am I then? And what will I do?"

The little girl pursed her lips and straightened the collar of her pink blouse. With his bulging eyes, the púca saw that the blouse had been fastened incorrectly, so a lone button waited at the top, forlorn. Her purple cotton skirt and pristine white tights looked new. Indeed a small tag peeked out from the waist of the skirt. *Strange child.*

"I don't have carrots. But if you're hungry, I have fudge. Ya want some?" Maeve retrieved her paper bag. It jangled. She withdrew a small, thin, white box that smelled faintly of brown sugar and peanut butter.

As he nodded, the rabbit's long ears bobbed. His cotton tail swayed. Maeve tossed the box at him. She sprinted off, her red Mary Janes hitting puddles and casting drips of mud onto her white tights as she ran.

Sweet. He chuckled, letting her go.

The next Tuesday, and the Tuesday after that, she returned, carrying with her a faded copy of *The Voyage of the Dawn Treader* peppered with ripped pages. The púca allowed her to walk one yard further into his fallow playground each time.

❧

One night, he wanted her coins and candy. Horned and half obscured, he crouched beneath a deflating, moss-coated climbing tire and held out his hairy palm. "Women's children speak riddles. You come here to fall down. Then you go to see Mr. Gile whom you say snaps at you like a ferret. If you're a bad girl like he says, Maeve, why does your tutor give you presents?"

She bit her lip. "I dunno. He wears fake red hair that smells funny. But Mama says he helps me with my reading, and he tutors out of the goodness of his heart."

Famished, the púca, in the form that night of a small, goat-headed pony, tossed Maeve's three chocolate Tootsie Roll Pops into his maw, wrapper, sticks, and all. With the toe of her white Keds, Maeve dug into the dandelions and dirt by the edge of the tire. Beyond that, taller and taller weeds choked the field in the gathering dark.

"You should be afraid."

"Of Mr. Gile?" she asked, blushing.

"Of me. But you're not."

A cloud shifted, and the only star Maeve knew, Cassiopeia, burst into view in the summer sky. Crossing her arms and puffing out her cheeks she declared, "If you eat me, no one will bring you money and lollipops." But her voice betrayed her by rising at the end, so the hungry spirit knew it was a question Maeve asked herself.

"You are a wise girl. Strange, but wise."

"Thanks."

"It is night now. Go. A child's mother will worry."

Maeve considered his yellow goat eyes. Suddenly, she smiled, waved, and skipped away on the path through the brush she had marked the week before.

The next Tuesday came and went. No children dared to cross the fetid mud ringing the deserted grasses that had attacked the former playground. By day, hawks circled. By night, owls hunted. Nearby motorists imagined they saw shadowy mares racing along the shoulder of Concord's roads. Mothers smelled garlic and dreamed of thunderstorms.

Maeve was sitting on her front steps looking with red-rimmed eyes at a new copy of *Number the Stars*.

"Where are you going, or not going, my friend?" The whiny voice of the squat, big-nosed hobgoblin in his hat of tree branches made Maeve jump half a foot in the air.

Wobbly, she landed at the edge of the middle stair. "Is it you?"

The wee, grinning bogeyman in the pointy shoes—carrying what appeared to be a small bundle of wheat—made a dancing bow. "Indeed!"

Maeve produced one plump, Red Delicious apple from the pink checked bag on her shoulder. "Sorry I didn't . . . here you go."

As she tossed her snack, the púca saw the spread of purple bruises across the child's right hand, knuckle, and fingers.

In one swift motion, the spirit stuffed the entire fruit into his wide mouth and chomped it to bits. He watched her.

Maeve studied her frilly socks. One fat tear escaped her eye.

Sniffing the air, he trotted around the house and regarded the empty driveway with concern. He closed his eyes for ten seconds, searching. Then, racing back in his long, pointed shoes, the púca hopped up onto the step next to Maeve. "Your mother starting taking an accounting class after work on Tuesdays, so Mr. Gile is coming here now."

Maeve nodded. She pointed above them to the blue ruffled curtains of the second-floor window of her bedroom. In his mind's eye, the púca could see her blue and purple polka dot bedspread and her collection of silver bracelets and rings embellished with jumping horses.

"He wants to read upstairs." Her tears fell in earnest.

A rusted green Chevy pulled around the corner and drove down the block.

"He's coming," Maeve sobbed.

"Don't read the wheat or eat the greens," the goblin sang. Then he threw his hands wide and sheaves of wheat flew about in every direction, seeming to multiply in the wind that suddenly roared for miles and miles. People all over town were temporarily blinded by whirls of grain.

Thunk! Mr. Gile's Chevy crashed into her neighbor, Mrs. Petticer's, freestanding, cast iron mailbox.

With a loud cackle, the púca goblin vanished in the grain

twister.

When the echo of her friend's laughter faded and her eyes cleared, Maeve saw Mr. Gile hop out of his car, adjust his slipping auburn toupee, and yell curses into his cell phone. Then wrinkled Mrs. Petticer strode out her front door into the still-blowing annual grasses and demanded to know what her mailbox had ever done to him! And furthermore, who was teaching men how to drive these days?

Maeve laughed, whispered "Thank You" into the air, bounded into her front hall, and locked the door behind her.

The following evening, a midnight-haired horse galloped across the town while cicada sang. As he moved, tiny seeds of wheat trailed from his velvety, dark mane. He came to a stop on the outskirts of the abandoned playground. In the moonlight, his silver eyes saw a small girl wearing white cotton pajamas embroidered with pink flamingos and a too-big Boston Red Sox cap spread a plaid blanket on the ground. On it, she laid out a rotisserie-roasted chicken, two baked potatoes, and a bag of Chips Ahoy cookies. When she finished setting out the feast, Maeve ran away barefoot.

❧

After his supper, the púca lay back and rubbed his gray, furry rabbit belly.

"One good turn deserves another," he said to the clover and weeds on the ground. "An insidious garden grows across town." The rabbit spat and dandelions withered and blackened all around him.

"Devils live in unremarkable houses." Sniffing and scrunching his nose, the rabbit caught no maleficent odors streaming from the back kitchen window of number thirty-six Curland Road—just a whiff of Kraft macaroni and cheese stuck to the bottom of a pot on the stove's burner. While rabbits lack a tapetum lucidum, the púca saw the sleeping Mr. Gile through the golden tapestries of his thoughts. Gile snored.

A moment later, a low sound flitted past Gile's ears, causing him to toss and turn in his squeaky bed. Groggy, he sat up and rubbed his bulbous, hairless scalp. The scents of charred bread and Allspice filled Gile's room. Again the low sound darted by him. Perhaps water coming out of a hose. Perhaps nothing. Gile blinked and lay his head back down on his sweaty pillow.

An image flickered behind his eyelids as sleep reclaimed him: a huge hare dancing about in Gile's vegetable garden, tramping on the peas and spitting at the tall vines of his tomato plants. An enchanted bow played a fiddle. Gile's snoring cut through the rousing tune.

Without witnesses, the púca kissed one withered, green tomato on the vine and then vanished into a school of fireflies swimming across the sky. The sun began to rise.

❦

After a bologna sandwich lunch the next day, Maeve's mother broke the news about poor Mr. Gile's unexpected death. Maeve counted the pink stripes on her favorite shorts so as not to smile.

"I knew it."

"Knew what?" Her mother asked, appraising her lovely girl. "What's got those wheels in your brain turning?"

Maeve dropped her gaze to her Mary Janes. "Some tomato plant leaves are poisonous. I saw it on TV."

"If only he'd known not to eat them. He studied so many books but misread his garden," her mother mumbled as she cleared the table. She downed a gulp of coffee. Then she led her daughter out into the yard for a game of badminton.

Maeve never saw her púca again but she often dreamt of him at daybreak, in the moments right before waking, when dreams feel alive.

The Stain of Caterpillars

All I heard was "accident" and "your brother."

The music vacuum had clued me in that something was wrong. There was no Carole King, no Don McLean, not even the Eagles, playing on the eight-track. I squinted over at my dad, but he was looking down at a single caterpillar defiling the steering wheel. Despite the breeze coming through his open window, his face and scalp shone with sweat. He wore his blue, button-down Oxford shirt and had removed his navy tie. Without mom to iron our clothes, all his shirts had waves of wrinkles down their sleeves.

From his seat beside me, he began to speak quietly about Jesus and heaven. I twisted my friendship bracelet on my wrist. My classmate, Kurt, and his pretty, blond mom raced past us in her red Mustang, and the Stones' voices blared into the air. I tapped my feet and fell into the baseline.

The week that followed blurred into hymns, awkward hugs from relatives, and constant wading through a wriggling sea of black suits. Right up until the family viewing, I just blinked, waved, and swayed. "Be Not Afraid . . . I go before you always." Timmy wasn't going anywhere. He ran faster and punched harder than any boy I'd met at Parker Middle School. When that fierce eighth grader, Ginger Watkins, pushed me down near the bike rack, Timmy demanded she "back off." My brother was too tough to die.

But I couldn't deny the white-skinned, stiff-fingered reality of Tim's open casket. Or the empty chair we set aside for my mom in the first row of seats. I asked my father if the gypsy moths would be crawling all over the ground at the cemetery. Whether there would be caterpillars in Tim's grave. Whether the moths had invaded the South, too, and could eat the palm trees outside mom's hotel. My dad frowned and patted the top of my head like he did with Erin, our Border Collie.

After the funeral service, he sent me to my Aunt Bridget's house for the night. I wanted to go home and get my Nikes, my diary with the brass lock, and Tim's jean jacket. But Dad kept driving.

Aunt Bridget gave me a hug and one of her long, soft cotton nightgowns. It smelled like flowers. I was wearing it when the yellow dial phone on the wall in the hallway rang. I peeked around the guestroom door and watched shock pinch my Aunt's face.

"For how long?" she asked.

Before she hung up, I knew my dad wasn't coming back for me.

Tan, winged gypsy moths laid egg masses on my aunt's picnic table. Caterpillars stained the trees black. Caterpillars fed on the bark. They fed on the sunlight. They fed on my fear.

Blood-red Geraniums

Every summer at Maplewood Farms, bees dip and rise as if spreading the story of Chico's disappearance. Irises wave in the wind. Lavender plants huddle and guard the secret.

"I don't know any Chico," Julian says.

In my mind, I still hear his words and wonder.

&

July heat rises off the metal hide of the coffee truck as if it were a silver armadillo. I squeeze into line behind the pickers, trying not to look at their brown, taut muscles as they buy bottles of juice or gnaw on sticks of beef jerky. Flushed, I stare instead at the caked black earth crawling up their work boots. My young-adult brain can't decide whether it is racist to think about how the Haitian guys wear muscles better than the Irish and Italian-American boys in my neighborhood. The owners have bussed pickers down from the fields in New Hampshire. Maplewood usually reflects enough of the idyllic fantasy of farm life to keep Ann-Taylor-wearing housewives flooding to the painstakingly-decorated farm stand and garden center, but, during a harvest, many hands must work the land. Fresh crops demand care, sweat, and blood.

From an old boombox adorned with a KISS 108 FM sticker that someone has left on the picnic table, Boyz II Men sing "End of the Road." Behind me in line, the head picker, Chico, holds his work radio like a microphone. He steals the chorus and weaves it into his own love song sung in a mix of Spanish and Haitian Creole. I turn to watch him and Chico bends in an exaggerated bow.

Danny cuts into line in front of me, nonchalantly holding *The*

Boston Herald under one arm. "Mau-reen, string bean," he says into my left ear. "Where you been all morning, Sunshine?" I blush. His ginger hair and goofy smile complement his freckles. The farm stand cashiers often say he's cute, in a Larry Bird kind of way.

"Hi! Boy, it's hot," I stammer. Why didn't I take the job at Express, folding skinny jeans? Why had I let my love of fresh air drive me into a mix of budding plants and teasing men?

The produce guys stroll over to Danny with a pizza and a six-pack of Coke. I am thwarted yet rescued by their argument about the best pitcher the Sox ever had. As the young men walk off together, I buy a turkey sandwich. Nausea churns in my stomach. I surrender my lunch to the wasps.

An hour later, I am calf-deep in Liberty Hosta in the green-house when Danny returns. I have nowhere to hide. My fingers peel off browning leaf after browning leaf and drop them into a yellow, plastic bucket. Relentless heat pounds down from the solar panels. As he balances a tray of blood-red geraniums about to sprout in one hand, Danny stops and blocks my path with his broad shoulders.

"So what do college girls do at night? Calculus? Read poetry?" His lips turn up at the corners.

I watch a fat drop of sweat slide down his neck and resist the urge to wipe it away for him.

"My mom is into Emily Dickinson. Dragged me all the way out to her museum," he continues with a laugh. "I pretended to hate it, but it was OK."

Green leaves and bright blooms form a cocoon around us. I inch closer. His musky smell draws me to him.

"You wetback shithead!"

We turn towards the shout and hear a grunt followed by a muffled cracking sound. I can't see much, but I imagine work boots connecting with bone.

"We'll get the berries in without you halfwits! Take your

Español and your Creole gibberish back to your own countries!" a man yells.

Gasping, I turn to Danny, but he has already set the budding perennials down and dashed through the open door. I sprint after him.

Rob, the landscaping manager, clasps a silver flask in his hands. Over and over his right foot cracks into Chico's swollen head. Writhing, Chico tries to ball himself up to protect against the blows.

"Stop!" Danny says.

Rob stumbles, drops his flask and lurches in Danny's direction. Despite being twice Danny's age and wobbling from drinking too much Wild Turkey, Rob manages to land a right-handed punch on Danny's upper arm. Janjak, the most experienced picker, starts to move towards the men.

"Back off. Pancho Villa is getting what he deserves," Rob slurs.

Instinctively, I hurry to Chico and cradle his head into my sweat-stained t-shirt. Trickles of blood roll down the Maplewood Farms crest.

"Are you all right? Chico? *Chico!*" A shrill voice rises, and I realize it's my own.

Cashiers abandon their registers and rush out of the stand as Rob shouts about hell and "bastard Mexican immigrants." Two cashiers debate whether to call the owners or the ambulance, and the other two argue about whether Chico comes from Colombia, El Salvador, or Mexico. Rob rushes Danny. Danny coldcocks him.

"Call . . ." I begin to yell to the group of cashiers, but falter. "Call 9-1-1!" Chico's head drifts to one side and his eyes glaze over.

A dusty Dodge Ram pickup screeches in, and Julian, the farm manager, jumps out. He gestures at Sully, the six-foot-two supervisor of the field workers, and at two muscular Hispanic men I do not recognize. Julian pulls me out of the way, and then he and the other two men descend on Chico and the fighters. I can't tell whether they are there to help, or harm, the fallen Chico.

Marcy, the head cashier, walks out of the stand, takes my arm and leads me, along with all the other young women, into the sweet-smelling fruit market.

"Ambulance?" I ask.

Moving her hand as if erasing a blackboard she says, "Wait."

We hear Julian's truck pull away. Looking out a window, I see that the plants in the yard are the only remaining witnesses. The twenty-foot journey to the payphone looks like a million-mile trek. I shiver. Mud and blood clump under my fingernails. Determined not to be the fragile college girl, I bite my lip and will myself not to cry.

"You'll be working in the shed. Wash and glove up and go box berries," Marcy says to me softly, her order an attempt at soothing.

"I'm on perennials."

"Not anymore," she says as the light drains from her eyes. "Don't worry. Julian will deal with this. He'll call the doctor, and the cops, if he has to. He handles trouble."

For the next two days, my gloved hands scoop plump strawberries into green boxes. Runts and squishers I set aside for my breaks. Each time, I stare at the payphone across the yard, wonder when Danny will return, and forget to eat them.

On the third day, a navy blue Crown Victoria rolls into the lot. A trim man with buzz-cut black hair walks past the open doors of the work shed, through the farm stand, and towards the office. Paramount Pictures' casting department could not have brought in a better police detective. Alone in my berry-stained refuge, I hold my breath. Curiosity pulls me into the fruit market to learn what's going on. A cashier named Jennifer stage-whispers to another cashier, Ali, who stage-whispers to the next one, the word "homicide." When the detective walks out again, I run to the tiny bathroom and throw up.

At the end of the shift, Julian calls all the employees out into the yard. His considerable bulk blocks my view of the payphone.

He breaks into his wide, family-farmer smile he usually reserves for tanned housewives shopping for fresh corn.

"Good work today, team," Julian says, wiping his sweaty brow with a blue bandanna. "So, you may have some questions, or hear other people asking questions, about the incident that happened with Rob a couple of days ago. We all need to be on the same page. To work here together." He pauses. "Since he was insubordinate and drunk on the job, I fired Rob. And Danny has a lot going on in his family, so he had to resign."

"Huhs?" and "Whys?" rise from the gathered workers.

"He said to tell Maureen and Jennifer goodbye," Julian continues. Someone in the crowd snickers and my cheeks burn. "Sad those two men had to go. Listen, if we are going to keep *working together*, we need to be clear on what happened."

No one responds to the implied threat. Julian rubs his chin and waits.

"Chico?" Janjak asks. The group of pickers around him murmurs in concern.

"I don't know any Chico," Julian says.

The Angels of Pont-Saint-Esprit

In her mercy, Mother ties me to a chair in the attic with rough, wheat-colored rope. Fishermen tell Mother that Monsieur Armunier writhes in his straightjacket, yelling about serpents upon him. Nurses and nuns rush to his aid. But mother does not trust me, *ma belle jeune fille*, to the doctors at the asylum, so we guard my secret at home.

The attic roof leaks. Raindrops kiss my cheeks.

Silvery lights flash and my stomach convulses. Delicate bells of lily of the valley wrap me in their sweet aroma. I am grateful. As flames crackle in the river, seraphim rise on blue-tipped wings. Their celestial voices join in a libretto of glory. I also sing. Then I ride the crescendo of sound to them. They enfold me in their wings of sky, and we soar and dip above the spreading fire.

"Quiet, child," my mother says.

No, I cannot have the bread, because it is cursed. No, I cannot have the water, because it is poisoned.

But I would eat any blight and drink any venom to dance with my angels again. I guard my vision as the poison retreats. Awaking from sleep, I feel the message of archangels beat in my chest. What can I achieve to be worthy of this gift? How will I share the triumph that my soul knows?

One day, I will burn past the Saturday market and across the twenty arches of the bridge. I will become my own miracle.

Historical Note: This piece was inspired by the 1951 mass-poisoning incident in the small French village of Pont-Saint-Esprit. Many local residents fell gravely ill and experienced hallucinations. More than forty people were interned at the local asylum where they were restrained in straight-jackets or chained to beds, and seven people died. Historians have proposed various theories about the mysterious incident, including ergot poisoning caused by the rye bread at the local bakery, mercury poisoning, mycotoxins, or a possible CIA experiment with weaponizing LSD.

In a drought year, I didn't expect to meet the drowned. Yet the Sirens found me. Green and tan hills kissed with irrigated vineyards rose outside my second-floor window, but four pale, bloated faces loomed over me in my hospital bed. The falls whirled in my ears. I gasped.

"All ours," whispered a bluish female form.

By the time I pulled myself and my spider's web of IV and medical lines upwards into a sitting position, the faces were gone. Beeping sounds crescendoed from the EKG machine. I smelled the Polo cologne of Jesus, my stocky male nurse, before I passed out.

ॐ

"I put the 'flash' in flash flood," I tried to drawl to the brothers, nieces, and aunts swarming into my hospital room like fire ants. They heard gags and burbles. So much for showing them my faculties remained intact. Assuming they did.

"Your brother is a very lucky man," Dr. Becker said. "Frankly, we were not sure when, or if, he would respond to stimuli and regain consciousness."

"What kind of damn fool dives into muddy water under the only black clouds we've seen all month?" Christophe said, puffing out his chest. He slipped in a small puddle of river water on the floor and grabbed the edge of my bed to steady himself.

"Don't mind Uncle Chris. What he means to say is that we all know the swift currents where the river flows into the park are very dangerous," my niece, Heidi, said through a strained smile.

"We are all very grateful the ranger fished you out in time, Uncle Will."

With one arm, Dr. Becker herded my relatives out of the room. "I am sure your uncle appreciates your concern, but now he needs his rest. Come, let us continue this discussion in the waiting room."

> ❧

The Sirens returned to my room during the eleven p.m. shift change. I heard nurses exchanging pleasantries and passing on instructions from hastily-written chart notes as the smell of rotting skin and algae filled my nose.

"All ours, all ours, all ours," sang the smallest of the apparitions. She clasped hands with her three ethereal sisters, and they swayed around my bedside.

"G-go away," I stammered.

"Swim with us. You're all ours."

A loud knock interrupted their eerie voices.

"Time for your medicine," said Judy, the cheerful, efficient overnight nurse, as she breezed into the room. Relief flooded over me.

"What's this?" Judy asked. She picked up a metal key. Fat drops of water fell from it onto my bedding. "Who could have left this behind?"

> ❧

Heidi never saw or heard them. They rolled me on the waves of their song every night at eleven. I could no longer blame the feel of their sopping, stringy hair on my hands on the fog of the many medications I had taken. I left the limestone hospital building behind, but the Sirens found me in my niece's cozy guest room. The doctors said my health improved every day, but they didn't know the truth. They never held a wet key in shaking hands. Dr. Weber prescribed thick sleeping tablets, but still my spectral choir sang.

⁊⋗

Two months into my recovery, I asked Heidi to retrieve my laptop from work.

"I need to check my insurance policy updates," I told her.

"We're working with Unity already, Uncle Will."

"I remember getting an email about changes in long-term benefits. It will only take ten minutes to check." Heidi raised an eyebrow. "I promise not to respond to emails. I won't overdo it."

Turning the mystery key over in my palm, I waited for my niece's return. I shuddered to think what Meyer had done to our office. He never filed. He hated temps. I'd bet my Horns' tickets that he drove around in his Lexus showing condos to UT coeds, ignored the mail, and rarely closed a deal. Any kind of deal.

"Here's your laptop and a cup of Echinacea tea. I'll peek back in here after *The Ellen Show*, and I expect you to be finished with both."

The metal of the laptop felt cool and reassuring in my hands. The screen glowed.

"Family of four, single mom. Come on, come on," I said to myself.

Fifteen minutes later, I found them. The Locke family. The two-acre plot and aging white ranch house south of the state park. I'd gotten them a good deal, hadn't I? I convinced the sellers to knock the price down $2,000 and even waived part of my commission. Anything to get rid of a fixer-upper so close to the floodplain. Rubbing my forehead with my left hand, I tried to summon up the buyer in my mind. Long, strawberry blond hair falling out of a careless ponytail. Freckles and a frown. I remembered her correcting me in a small, desperate voice that she answered to Ms. and not Mrs. That title, the way she clutched her battered hobo bag to her chest, her frequent glances at her daughters, and the blue shadow of a bruise on her cheek made me wonder if she and her girls were running from something. Or someone.

So what if I'd rushed through the required flood warning speech? It was all in the closing paperwork. If she didn't read it carefully before she signed, whose fault was that? I left her with the key to the ranch house and my standard goodbye line: "Here are the keys to your new tomorrow. It's all yours."

Memories returned to me, and I slumped back onto my pillows. The paper. I'd been two glasses into a bottle of Terra Vine's peppery 2015 Syrah when I'd read the news. I sat on the winery balcony and read *The Record Courier* over my charcuterie board.

"Family Drowned in Late Night Flash Flood," read the headline. Something about the woman pictured in the grainy black and white picture looked familiar. One of Meyer's women? Someone I'd met tailgating at UT? A client? *That* client? The sickening acidic taste rising from my throat could not be blamed on tannins.

❧

The clock blared a warning: ten p.m. already. Sweat trickled over me. I pressed my hands over my eyes.

"6332 0981. 0918? Damn it," I muttered. Before my accident and two-month nap at HCMC, Meyer and my family had raved about my head for numbers. Now, remembering my Visa Card number seemed like solving a quadratic equation. I looked at the clock. No time for pride.

"Heidi! Where are you? Come in here, please. Can you bring me my wallet?"

"What is it, Uncle Will? Here's your wallet and a cup of Chamomile." She shoved the steaming mug at me.

"Can you find something for me online?"

"Sure," she said, cocking her head. "How can I help?"

"Google the women's shelter. I want to make a donation for... Women's History Month."

A minute later, Heidi pulled up a site featuring a logo of a butterfly rising from a split heart. I clicked the "Donate" tab. Heidi watched as I charged a $1,000 donation to Austin's Safe Haven to my Visa card.

"That's very nice of you," she said, withdrawing my laptop from my grasp and patting me on the shoulder. "Women's History Month isn't until March, but I'm sure they always need money."

I slept. Neither the scent of wet moss nor the wretched singing of ghost girls disturbed me. The sun streaming through the window blinds woke me up at seven the next morning. I smiled. I barely noticed the small puddle of muddy water on the floor beside my bed.

&

I made my donations into a ritual. My philanthropic shamanism occurred every evening. Small donations to shelters across the country. I even sent Heidi to get Huggies when I read about the Methodist Church's diaper drive for Safe Haven.

"I don't know what's come over you, Uncle Will," she said, plopping the extra-large bag of Overnites on her kitchen table. "Have you always been this generous, and I just never noticed?"

"I need to repay . . . I need to pay . . . I need to get out of the house. I'll come along as you deliver these to the church. It's only three. There's plenty of time."

"Sure you feel up to it?"

I nodded and lugged the bulky bag of diapers to the car. Under my thin arm, it felt as heavy as a dead tree. On the way back from the old limestone church, I convinced my niece to turn right at the brown sign and take a detour through the state park. We signed in at the kiosk and drove a few miles down the dusty gravel road to the ranger station. Cacti thrived. Record winter heat broken by scant rains left trees parched and shrubs browning.

"Afternoon. It's a great day to be outdoors. How can I help y'all?" state park ranger Ted McCain said. He approached us in front of the station as I extracted myself from the passenger side of Heidi's Ford Fiesta.

"You don't recognize me. I'm Wilhelm Banes. You saved my life! I don't know how to thank you. I don't remember much from that day. I started out hiking. I'm not much of a swimmer, but I must have gone in, and when the water pushed me downstream, they say you saved me."

"Wow! You're the guy the water swept away from the banks near the falls." He shook my hand. "Sure good to see you up and around. I heard you were in a coma."

"He was," Heidi broke in. "Which is why he needs to thank you properly and get back in the car so I can get him right back home to a hot bowl of my chicken stew."

"Thank you, sir." My voice broke and my eyes welled up as I looked at the young, tall ranger.

"Glad to be of service. I'm so happy to see you made it. I saw a flash of your red jacket on the boulder abutting the bank and—"

"And?" I asked.

"Well, the rain was coming up suddenly. Lord knows we needed it, but the river churned and swelled so fast, and the sky changed so quickly as the clouds came in, it was hard to keep things straight. For a minute, I thought I saw you and some girls. But it was a trick of the light. It was only you. Good thing too. I never could have dragged five people out of there."

"Five?" My face drained of color.

"That's what I thought I saw. Four girls behind you on the

bank. 'Course, I blinked and realized it was only you, and I needed to get a pole and get you out before you ended up in Blanco."

I fell back against the car. McCain and Heidi opened the passenger side door and helped me into my seat. She waved at him as we drove away. Ignoring Heidi's objections, I rolled the window halfway down to feel the air on my face. A cold wind blew by us. In the trees by the side of the road, I glimpsed a blur of white as a rabbit hopped away. A hawk circled above. As we rounded the last curve to leave the park, the Siren's song echoed in the breeze.

"Still ours, still ours, still ours."

Kit-Cat Clock

The wide-eyed Kit-Cat Clock on the wall smiled down, the only witness. The cat saw the mouse-quiet way The Bastard pretended to look at candles in the back until Sylvia, a Monday night regular, left. I listened to the wind hissing against the front windows. But the cat caught the beady eyes under The Bastard's greasy Red Sox cap.

The Bastard came at me in the front of the store. He grabbed my left wrist. While I leaned towards the counter, trying to slam my right hand down on the red alarm button next to the register, The Bastard made a fist and clocked me good on the right side of the head. Sounds got muffled. Warm blood trickled out of my right ear. Then he crashed me onto the floor.

I tried to claw him off the buttons of my jeans, but his gloved hands swatted mine away. He pinned both of my arms back. Then I bit my lip and waited. The Bastard couldn't go on forever. The cat watched. I focused on not thinking about skin on skin, and concentrated on the gray opposite of thinking. Meanwhile, the cat's small, white second hand twitched.

Eventually, The Bastard rolled off me, stood, jimmied the register open, emptied the cash drawer, and took off. The cat saw me gather up my jeans and pull myself up to stand. Drops of blood and sperm dripped down my inner thighs. Time shifted. My legs refused to work. Wrapped in the cloud of The Bastard's musky stink, I froze for maybe five—or maybe thirty-five—minutes. Then I dragged myself out, drove home in my Chevy, and showered him off of me.

The next day, Detective Virginia Dubois brought me a Styrofoam cup of weak coffee. Could I identify him? The lack of physical evidence would cost me. She couldn't make any promises.

Driving home, I wondered what cops promised the ponytailed UNH girls, the moms with Lego pieces in their pockets, the librarians carrying *The Norton Anthology of Nice*. As the PTA types whispered, I'd been around. Not a lot of single, white moms with brown-skinned babies north of Manchester. Three consecutive stoner poets had been in and out of my one-bedroom before they went back on the road. A leather skirt and a bad-girl-with-a-heart-of-gold wink kept my landlord amused and my rent under nine hundred a month, but hadn't won me any friends. Never heard back from Virginia.

Two Monday nights later, I went back to work with an old Swiss Army Knife in the pocket of my new Goodwill Levi's. With a kid at home, I had to be practical. The wide-eyed Kit-Cat Clock on the wall smiled down, the only witness. At closing time, I pulled the cat down and smashed it.

I didn't need a witness. Nobody saved me. *No* body could. I had to be my own ally.

Aftershock Angels

Inside and outside, the earth quivers and quakes. My sister is with me, even after all these years.

Sweet Jarvis from State Indemnity has joined us for Chamomile tea in our good Royal Albert cups—the ones with the pink flowers—but then he decides to go talk to his associate, who is assessing upstairs. Busy boys, to call on a Tuesday evening. Sammy clomps downstairs, grabs a very large black bag, crosses the room and turns up my radio. Jarvis returns. He sits calmly and quietly, sucking the dark chocolate layer off the biscuits and putting the shortcake layer covered in spit back on the plate.

I know it is Tuesday evening because Lisa calls during their visit. Jarvis looks impatient, drums his fingers on his plate, wouldn't want to break it, but he must be a busy man. As usual, I am too busy for Lisa's rambling. She asks me, again, to move to Florida with them. She always calls between *First News at Five* and *Wheel of Fortune*, but before *Masterpiece Mystery*.

"I'm not moving."

"Come on, mom. It's dangerous up there. It's all over *The Weather Channel*. And we found the cutest condo! Pets allowed. Partial water view, even."

"Around here?"

"Listen, Abe and I worry about you. All alone up there except for your cat. Ever since Aunt Bea was called home—"

"Not interested," I say. "Bea is still with me."

"How have you been feeling? Are you taking your pills?"

"I'm not an idiot, girl. Rain's coming. Put sweaters on my grandsons," I say and hang up.

The couch sits further from the wall than it did yesterday. My right calf burns, burns until I plop down and prop my leg up on the embroidered, green pillow. Where is that clicker? Bea hides everything. I wrestle a bulky rectangle from the space between the faded cushions. I point and push, point and push. Nothing happens. I open the back of the remote and change the direction of the batteries. Positive becomes negative, negative becomes positive, and everything ekes out one more drop of juice. The TV screen blazes. Bingo!

"Daughter calling?" Jarvis asks, strolling over to the couch.

"Daughter-in-law. Thick as molasses."

"Good job. Just stay calm." He gives the slightest of nods towards the receiver curled up in the cradle as if ready to spring.

"As a cucumber. I'm staying put. I could never leave Bea alone here. But that silly mule, Lisa, just keeps asking."

Soon my nice visitor and I are watching my program. Because the chubby schoolteacher is too chicken to solve the puzzle, I lose interest. Then that infernal alarm goes off that means some poor girl has been kidnapped. I don't look up to read the text of the Amber Alert scrolling across the screen. I never notice cars, so I wouldn't be able to help. I could read that romance with the half-naked man on the cover, the one Mrs. Lemming dropped over, but my glasses have been hiding from me since the weekend. Sunday, probably. I weigh the comforting clarity of my Pearl Vision readers vs. the nerve tingle that will build and crest into a roar when I stand up. Bea will know where they are.

I slurp from a half-full can of Coke sitting on a neatly stacked pile of newspapers on the coffee table. I drink that weak herbal tea, and a little caffeine won't kill me, no matter what that homely doctor says. Jarvis startles me by standing up. He walks through the living room, feels his way past the small painting in the antique brass frame on the wall, and asks to use the bathroom. I begin to remind him about his muddy boots, but a coughing fit seizes me. He can find his own way.

Why do I hear bells? Did I leave something in the microwave? Minutes dart. My coughs wander away. Demanding, the phone rings on and on. "Yeah, yeah, I'm coming," I mutter. Patsy Cline's still singing and heading out "Walking After Midnight" in the kitchen, so I guess I left the radio on. Or Bea did.

"You feel it?" A voice asks over the scratchy landline.

"What? Who the devil is this?" I spit on the floor.

"Alice, it's me, Sandy Lemmings. Everything okay? Anything fall down over there?"

"Nothing fell. I'm as okay as I'm going to be with this dampness creeping over the entire valley."

"So you didn't feel the aftershock? The earthquake is all over the news."

I sigh. "Do you mean I have to go stand in the damn doorway again? Good Lord. My tuckus is killing me."

"No, radio news says it's over. Just a little one here, bigger down by L.A."

"Good. It was on the radio? And not the TV?"

"I saw an emergency weather alert on channel eight. Can you hear your TV okay?" Mrs. Lemmings pauses. "Want me to come over and check on all your paintings and shelves for you?"

"I must have dozed off. Two young men already came to help. I'm fine. Bea's fine," I hang up. I yawn.

I get a pencil and the cheap, orange spiral bound notebook Dr. Horseface gave me during my last appointment. He wrote "Sleep Log" and "Day, Month, Year" in tall, dark letters, in different columns, on the first page of lined paper. All the other lines stood bare. He creased the page, just slightly to separate the columns.

"Tuesday," I write, "Slept during my program." My t's waver and my d's droop.

Bump. I turn and look for the cat, Esther, or my sister behind me, but I find Jarvis. He's standing behind the couch, holding an empty brass frame, and frowning. The kitchen door slams and I remember his associate—Timmy or Sammy. My right ear starts to ache.

"We should be going now, ma'am," Jarvis says. White slivers of light pop out around his silhouette in the dim room.

"In this dark, I would think so." I manage a smile just before the linoleum shifts beneath me. I fall. My head throbs. An antique Wedgewood pitcher crashes down from its shelf.

"Hey, what's the holdup? What if there's a biggie, a real earthquake?" Sammy asks, tromping down the stairs. He lugs a heavy bag and wears my best purse, black leather with a real gold buckle, on one shoulder.

Jarvis does not answer. Is he frowning at me? My eyes pull themselves further and further down. Is the young man looking at me or the pitcher that also fell on the floor?

"Time's ticking. No safe. I already checked the freezer and under the mattress. Maybe check for coffee cans in the basement? With these Great Depression grannies, you don't need a mask, but you never know where they've stashed their green."

"Fine," Jarvis says.

I moan.

"You okay, lady?" nice, young Jarvis whispers.

When I open my eyes and remove the cool cloth someone has placed on my forehead, Jarvis stands alone in the living room. The front door has blown open again. Jarvis stands by the roll-top desk and waves something white in his hand.

"So did you want our senior plan? State Indemnity backs us, and that's why we came. " Jarvis looks down at his hand, and the paper, no, the envelope he is holding. "That's why we came, right, Mrs. Primrose? Mrs. Primrose?"

My eyes push themselves closed. Sweet sleep. I sway slightly. But he is still out there. I open my eyes and look towards him. "What are you selling again?"

"Life insurance." He is clutching a velvet pouch in his hand, the kind you'd get at the jewelers. My patched tabby cat slinks in the open door, sees the strange man, and dives under the kitchen table.

"Not tonight, dear. Thank you anyway—"

"Call me Sam." Jarvis pockets the envelope, walks to the door and puts his hand on the doorknob. The right side of his face creases upward in a lopsided grin. "I'll come back then. Thanks for the Fig Newtons." He pauses. Then after a second, he shouts, "Thanks for everything, ma'am, but we have to go back to the office now."

He waits. When his friend does not appear, he murmurs, "Take care, ma'am." He leaves something black on the floor, pushes the button on the back doorknob, and shuts the door behind him. Such nice manners. Rare these days.

Patsy, or Bea, sings "Your Cheatin' Heart" as I doze off again.

By the time I manage to get up and back to the table, neither of my young guests remains. Time to tidy up. I see a brass frame on the floor. Hopefully, the painting my father gave me wasn't damaged. Before I make it into the parlor to check, dizziness grabs me, sways me, then releases me; we waltz to a country twang.

One of the flowered plates tremors. I change course, stumble to the table, and grab it for support. But then the earth's vibrations flow out just as quickly as they flowed in. From the TV in the living room, concerned male voices rise with authority. I pick up the plate with my left hand and slowly trace the border with two fingers. No chips. I put the plate back down. Not so bad.

A door thuds closed. Another thud follows, louder. The thieving salesman falls.

I putter over to the cellar door, ignoring the ache that has returned to my ear. I pry the door open and look down the stairs. Squinting, I see a twisted lump halfway down the steps. It could be a dead dog, except for the big open green eyes and mop of human hair. And his neck twisted at an odd angle. Aftershocks have caused worse. Then I see my black purse laying there. Is that the insurance agent's nice friend? Is that—no it couldn't be—a gun? It must be a reflection in the dim light. I have to stop watching that NCIS program with the handsome actors.

Bea hums "Crazy." It's always been her favorite song. A sharp winter breeze, ice-kissed like the Colorado days of our girlhood, whips up the stairs of our California retirement house. I catch a glimpse of white fluttering in the cellar. Could be laundry on the dryer rack. Could be the faint shadow of my sister's thin frame, swaying as she sings.

Smiling, I shut the door and hum to myself. I feel steadier on my feet and make it to the couch fine. Queen Esther wriggles out from her hiding place beneath the sofa and rubs her furry, black body against my shins. "There's our good kitty," I tell her. She meows.

Using the clicker, I turn the volume down on all those smug professors and that dandy hosting the quiz show. I feel a dull pang, and then a quick spasm in my rump. Damn little pills Doctor Know-It-All gives me do diddly squat.

"Mrs. Primrose! Mrs. Primrose!" The busybody from next door raps on the back door. I lean back on the couch and tilt my head back on the pillow. I fake a snore, two snores, three. Queen Esther jumps up and curls up next to me. She purrs.

"Are you OK? A white van was parked in your driveway, and then it took off. Is everything all right in there?" Mrs. Lemming shouts.

The knocking and prattling continue, but I pretend not to hear. My ears are full of my sister's clear alto, and I can almost see her snapping her fingers along to "I Fall to Pieces."

The phone rings, and I'd bet every dollar I have in the cookie jar that it's Lisa again with her whiny voice and real estate listings. As if the kitty and I could leave my sister and move to some palm-tree town. The phone rings four times and then my answering machine picks up.

I close my eyes. I don't want to talk to anyone. There has been enough commotion today already. Inside and outside, the earth quivers and quakes. My sister is with me, even after all these years.

Plunge

Cloaked in cool refuge from the heavy pressing air of AUGUST writing itself across Texas in capital letters, I float. My black swim dress flows in the lap, lap of the waves like a cape, and I become an aquatic superhero—Wonder Wave Woman.

Why won't you swim? I want to tell you that the brown water smells like fertile algae replicating, replicating, and commanding its space. Once you wade in, away from the judgment of the steel ladders at the YMCA pool, the water shields you from the glare of the smooth muscles women are supposed to have had before they had children. Having never birthed a child, I have no excuse. I'm just fat.

The sunscreen you hate dissolves in microscopic bubbles the longer you stay submerged. I need to reapply. Do you? I push through to the surface, ashamed that I don't know how often to nag you to slather cream on your golden skin. Precious to me.

"Run in. Stop squealing," I call. Not to quiet you, but because the waves are alive with sound. Run in. It's briny joy to float.

Marked

Joan emerged stamped with fire. No wonder the doctors called her birthmark "Nevus flammeus." Seconds later, Flora broke through unscathed. Flora let out a cry. The doctor and nurses exhaled.

❧

When her mother, Portia, brushed young Joan's hair in the morning, she looked at the port-wine colored, tongue-like mark on her daughter's face with widened eyes and arched eyebrows. Joan never knew if those eyes were full of fascination or fear. Her sister, Flora, trotted off to preschool wearing braids tied with sparkly blue elastics or satiny red ribbons. But their mother clipped two-dollar brown barrettes in Joan's hair and finished with her as quickly as she could.

From the bold primary colors of preschool to the polished wood panels of the university, Joan's twin walked next to her, wanting to cover her gently, like snow. When two high school bullies, Jack and Matt, called Joan "inkblot ugly," Flora quietly exposed that they had been copying her math tests over her shoulder all year. Then Flora parked her used sedan too close to them in the school parking lot and *accidentally* opened her doors into the sides of their red spoiled-boy convertible sports car. Never bully a twin.

Despite Flora's protective embrace of her sister, breath catches in Americans' throats when anyone as different as Joan walks by. So Joan was pushed past the margins years before she learned to resist.

Blaine met her at Congressman Bask's office—one of the wave of fired-up moms and frightened looking twenty-something men who came to complain about Bask's vote to repeal the Health Care Innovation Acts. They filled the green pleather seats. Blaine tried to speak with all the constituents in a patient tone of voice, but sometimes he wished he could play them a video. Perhaps one in which his doppelganger explained that the senator was not in, and was not expected in Texas anytime soon. Then Robot Blaine would calmly jot down their comments.

Blaine knew he shouldn't complain. He had to borrow his mom's car, but his boss had offered Blaine the small parking space next to the dumpster. He never had to buy his own office supplies. His girlfriend, who worked part-time as a barista at Starbucks, kept reminding him that he "was lucky to have the internship. A whole pack of Poli-Sci students applied, dude."

Still, he shrugged into his Ford Focus every night craving a beer. The weight of the day's complaints pushed his shoulders down.

After his nightly sub sandwich and beer, he took to taking down the framed, black-and-white photograph of his father shaking hands with Ronald Regan. He studied his father's eyes.

"Right first and loyalty second," he had told Blaine once, as he dressed in his finest suit and Yale tie for a fundraiser. The air felt heavy at Bask's office, and Blaine's chest never swelled with either justified optimism or fidelity. There were always donor requests to send and red-faced constituents to meet. Pragmatism ruled the day.

When his sister in Atlanta called each Sunday night, she spoke about her administrative job at Habitat for Humanity in proud tones. You could almost hear her smile floating from the cell phone towers.

"My pastor found me a true blessing, sending me here." She'd say, "Blaine, you don't need a job, you need a calling."

He would sigh, hang up, pour himself a beer, and turn on *The Walking Dead*.

⁊⸱

The first time he saw her, Joan startled him. She happened to sit next to the spot where Senator Bask's daughter, Candice, leaned against the wall. Candice stared at her smartphone and wore her patented sneer. She'd have to wait until five past five to ask after her father. To inquire before that would be a confirmation that the senator was, in fact, working in his office behind a cadre of interns and staff. Joan approached Blaine's desk.

"I need to see my senator."

"I'd be happy to—" Blaine said.

"Probably not happy, but you will. Bask and his friends cut off my insurance." He lowered his eyes at the sight of her siren birthmark, but they landed on the snarl of her lip, and he didn't like that much either. He wondered if she wanted to try to have that Gorbachev thing removed from such a large area of her face. If she was uninsured, she'd never be able to pay for laser surgery anyway.

"I'm not going away just because he doesn't want to see me."

"I'm sorry but the senator is not in today—"

"Listen!" She grabbed his forearm. "I don't care where he is, he doesn't want to *see* me."

"Um, is there a specific message you would like me to pass on?" He wriggled away from her.

"I can't afford to see my doctors now, so the sunset is coming. Gold until the dark."

"Well, the senator wants everyone to have access to health care choices, but in a sustainable, practical way—"

"I didn't choose the gold. Or the dark. They chose me."

She stood and waited for the answer to an unasked question. Damned if Blaine knew what to say. Then another woman whisked in, almost identical to Joan but brighter and softer, as if she had sprung to life from a social media filter. She tilted her head and revealed her porcelain skin.

"Shame on you for deserting my sister," Flora said to him. She looked around at the well-appointed office and peach-skinned staffers wearing white or navy dress shirts. "Who needs the most help? People like her who are already sick. People who live precariously every day, so the docs on call don't always see their emergencies. And then your politicians grab away what help she has. Shame on all y'all!"

Blaine wondered what his own sister would say to them. Her heart always found words for her mouth.

Flora led Joan across the office and out the door. Their anger lingered in the air behind them, like a cigarette smell.

He dreamt of the birthmark girl that night. He awoke in his small apartment on Washington Street to a vague, cobb-web-like memory of her running down a narrow alley. He shook the dream off and went looking for the Starbucks Sumatra beans his girlfriend always brought over. But the birthmark girl's stained face loomed in his mind. Her name. What had she said her name was?

The better the wine, the more devoted the members of the Democratic Ladies' Society became, but, since the election of an unpredictable Independent leader, a good crowd attended no matter what the spread. Portia Harper slid a rust-colored ceramic plate of baked Brie and store-brand nine-grain crackers onto her coffee table next to the large, silver-framed portrait of her daughter Flora in front of her nursing school. Portia fingered her pearls and nodded along as her friends discussed possible alliances. She cranked up the A/C when asked and tried not to think about her electric bill.

"Dana and her young women at NARAL— their hearts are in the right place carrying the torch of Roe versus Wade—but really they are too shrill. Shrill doesn't sell," Retired attorney Elizabeth Price said with a frown.

The group's facilitator, Diana Chan, took a deep breath. "In the current climate, we all need to come together, find common ground, and move forward—"

"Yelling and throwing tampons at the governor never won anyone any friends," Ms. Price replied.

"And it's disgusting. There has to be a way to advance the cause in a nicer fashion." Dorothy Crowes straightened her floral silk blouse.

"These are serious issues, ladies. We need an ongoing, realistic action plan and allies if we want to make a difference," said Diana.

"What lovely appetizers, Portia. I always say buffets are much too heavy for a mid-evening meeting. How's your Joan, bless her heart?"

Portia shifted in her chair. "Still painting. She's in a group show next month. Determined to keep working hard. But she . . . follows her own path."

"Where is she living now?"

"More chardonnay?"

Laura, an unconvincingly blond real estate agent, leaned over and whispered to Dorothy, "They don't talk. Heard she was barely scraping by, poor girl. Who could live off what an artist makes? But she's too proud to quit working and take disability. Can you imagine?"

"Ahem . . . well, Portia must be refusing to enable Joan's eccentricities. Forcing her to earn her own way."

Laura nodded and scanned the room, bypassing the inherited

art to note the cracked plaster on the baseboards and the remnants of a purplish stain on the Turkish carpet. The kind of stain one would need a professional cleaning to remove. She saw that the award-winning chardonnay came from the Texas Hill Country, not Côte de Beaune in Burgundy. A smile tugged at her lips as she wondered how soon Portia might have to put her craftsman bungalow on the market.

§

Joan and Flora waited amongst a seething sea of protestors in front of the university. They hoisted signs ranging from "Support Texas Families - Support Healthcare" to "Your Lies Don't Represent Me" to "Bask out in 2020!" One young man's sign included a hand-drawn picture of Bask's head on a Kraken attacking a ship full of women and children.

"Extra points for creativity," Flora said to the bearded artist. He beamed.

Despite the university's promise that the Weekend Lecture Series was free and open to the public, a corps of burly security officers checked each person waiting outside for a university ID. Only current students and faculty were allowed within twenty-five feet of the auditorium. Joan's expression flattened and Flora hated to leave her to go to her study group.

§

The metal of the heavy, rust-splotched gas can bumped against the purple cluster of spider veins on her Joan's shin as she lugged it across the alley. She hoped she'd remembered to throw her insulin and Zoloft in the trash can, but she couldn't be sure. If the story became about her pills, it would be easier for Bask to block his ears. A plump, sniffing rat darted out the back door of a posh brasserie as Joan turned the corner and walked around the block.

Her watch read 6:55 am. The night security officer took his last pass down the street in his light blue sedan.

When Joan reached the graffiti on the sidewalk in front of the door to Bask's office, she set the gas can down. She checked her watch and waited. "He's late" she mumbled and then began to hum. At 7:00 a.m., she left a voicemail telling her sister that she loved her, and then called in a tip to the KHOU news line.

At 7:15 a.m., Blaine was the first person to enter the office through the back door. Fred, the staffer in charge, slept on the couch in his office per usual. Bask's Aggie buddy for twenty years, he never seemed bitter that his friend didn't promote him to the DC office. Blaine pulled up the shades as he drank his coffee—bitter and weak, no comparison to Sumatra Gold—and saw the security guard ambling down the sidewalk to reach his post, twenty minutes late.

His post where someone already stood. Blaine could only see the woman from the back, but his fingers tensed and he knew, in the silly way witnesses always tell the female news reporter that they just *knew*, it was the girl with the birthmark. The girl took a rectangular object, her phone probably, and placed it on a thin plastic stand.

"No! Shit no!" he thought as she lifted the red can and doused herself with gasoline. Even though the girl couldn't hear him, Blaine banged and banged on the window glass.

"No!" he yelled at his reflection.

Joan dropped the can and raised a single match. "Bask lies," she said in a matter-of-fact tone to the video recording on her phone and the frozen security guard. Three teens biking to school slowed, looked for the source of the gasoline smell. Two stopped, hit their kickstands, and pulled out their cell cameras without saying a word.

"Call 9-1-1! Call 9-1-1!" Blaine yelled through the glass. His work landline lay poised next to his list of major campaign donors on his desk, but Blaine's heavy legs wouldn't carry him that far.

Though he could not have heard, a pimpled boy in an Astros cap pulled over behind his friends, lifted his smartphone, and did exactly that. His peers clicked away.

When flames darted at her eyes like a snake's tongue, Joan let out one gurgling cry. Then she lurched and fell.

§

Joan's scorched face floated across social media. She became a monster, or a martyr, depending on one's point of view.

They called her birthmark a stain.

Blaine slipped down the glass and sat on the office floor next to the window. He pulled his name badge off his shirt and crushed it beneath his twice-worn loafers. He submitted his resignation via text. As soon as the ambulance and cops cleared out that night, Blaine cleared off his desk and marched out of Senator Bask's office and his political party. Bask might creep away from Joan's recrimination in a week or a month or a year. Outrage would stain her friends and family forever.

On Election Day, Flora gathered every nurse and student she could reach. They stood one hundred and one feet from the busiest polling place in the city holding a painted banner reading, "Vote for Healthcare Access." Linking arms, they swayed like waves in pink, blue, and pastel-spotted scrubs. As they moved, they repeated Joan's name like an appeal. Then like a command. Then like a hymn.

THE END

THANK YOU, KIND REVIEWERS

Now that you have finished *Enduring Spirit*: *Stories* (The Cross-roads Collection #2), please consider leaving an honest review on Amazon, Goodreads, Litsy, or your favorite book blog. Reviews are the most direct and concrete way to help authors like me reach new readers. I would be truly grateful! If you do write a review, please email me via my publisher at editor@spiderroad-press.com so that I can thank you.

Special Reader's Bonus
Excerpt from *Trail Ways Pilgrims: Stories*

(The Crossroads Collection #1)

The Wisdom of Oranges

I took on nick-names, Genna, then Evie, because expats can. In hiking group, they called me Mrs. Genevieve. When he woke up sleepy-eyed and headachy next to me, lean, sarcastic Matt called me his partner in crime. Words like "Honey," "Baby," and "girl-friend" hung elusive in the moist air between us, never descending.

In his black messenger bag, I'd seen a gold heart necklace engraved with the word "love" and the English nickname of his Korean tutor. The young woman with the lustrous, long, straight black hair. Yet in the fifteen quiet minutes between my first alarm and the snooze button reminder, Matt would pull his tanned arms around me and we'd spoon, needing no words at all.

We set off. The early morning air bit at my cheeks.

"What I wouldn't give for two weeks away," Matt muttered.

Mist clung to my boots and the frayed edges of my jeans. I had not been able to find a pair of the requisite black hiking pants that fit. The width of my hips confounded the eager salesgirls. Size 98? Size 100? I had bowed my thanks and marched off. I would never consent to wear any item sized 100, even if they were the last pair of pants in this crowded, pungent, sparkling city. Jeans would do.

"Come to New Brunswick with me for the spring break," I said.

Wrapped in brume, I rubbed the wooly palms of my mittens together. I created friction.

Matt slid a slim, red pack of cigarettes out of his coat pocket and then studied his hiking boots.

"We're lost," he said.

"Like figuratively?"

"We've been waiting here a while, and the other cars haven't

47

arrived." Matt looked up, pulled out a white filtered cigarette and put it between his lips.

I arched one brow.

"So?" My invitation home had slipped out, but once offered, it crackled between us like the thick, nervous air after a lightning storm...

Want to continue reading *Trail Ways Pilgrims: Stories* (The Crossroads Collection #1)? See: http://spiderroadpress.com.

Acknowledgements

I would like to thank my wonderful son, who inspires me every day. I owe gratitude and a sushi dinner to my patient husband. Thanks to Gay Yellen, Pamela Fagan Hutchins, Jody T. Morse, Violet Moore, my fellow SRP writers, Jennifer Morales and Francizka Voeltz, my beta readers, everyone at writing group, and the gals from Lexington. Mary Ellen and Karen, my solid and hilarious sisters, where would I be without you?

I give my special thanks to you, dear reader, for accompanying me on this literary journey.

ABOUT THE AUTHOR

Patricia Flaherty Pagan is a talkative introvert who likes reading and writing about tenacious women. She is the author of *Trail Ways Pilgrims: Stories* (The Crossroads Collection #1) and *Enduring Spirit: Stories* (The Crossroads Collection #2). She is the editor of *Up, Do: Flash Fiction by Women Writers*, *Approaching Footsteps*, *In The Questions*, and *Eve's Requiem,* as well as a writer of award-winning literary and crime short stories. Pagan teaches creative writing in Texas. In 2013, after receiving her MFA in Creative Writing from Goddard College, she founded Spider Road Press. She is pretty sure she adopted the world's coolest kid. Learn more about her on her website: www.patriciaflahertypagan.com.

Patricia loves her book group, and would enjoy speaking to yours. She facilitates workshops about short fiction, women's issues in literature, writing about violence effectively, and small press publishing. If you would like her to present at your book group, conference, or convention, contact her via Spider Road Press at editor@spiderroadpress.com.

OTHER BOOKS BY SPIDER ROAD PRESS

Trail Ways Pilgrims: Stories
(The Crossroads Collection #1)
By Patricia Flaherty Pagan

Moving short stories and flash fiction from award-winning author Patricia Flaherty Pagan. How far would you go to become a mother? To find love? To leave your loss behind? Experience five haunting glimpses into the lives of women confronting hard choices in settings ranging from the lush tropics to misty mountaintops to snowy cities. Available from the Spider Road Press website bookstore and on Amazon.com.

Approaching Footsteps:
Four Suspenseful Novellas
Written by
Rita Banerjee
Donna Hill
Jennifer Leeper
Megan Steusloff

Four compelling novellas add up to one suspenseful and entertaining collection! Best-selling novelist Donna Hill spins a gripping tale of desperation and danger. Author Jennifer Leeper puts a unique spin on noir fiction. In a tale of murder and magic, author & scholar Rita Banerjee blends a story of two unlikely allies trapped in a monsoon with a tale of murder and magic. Writer Megan Steusloff contributes a story of historical suspense. Complex characters and vivid settings drive these powerful narratives. Bonus flash fiction fascinates. It's available on Spiderroadpress.com, in select bookstores, and on Amazon.

In the Questions: Poetry by and about Strong Women

Edited by Patricia Flaherty Pagan and Kessika Johnson

Questioning is liberating, challenging, surprising, and can be both painful and beautiful. Explore these poems and step into the questions with us. Featuring poetry by award-winning and emerging poets such as Andrea Barbosa, Candace Bergstrom, Donna Hill, Teresa Mei Chuc, Patricia Flaherty Pagan and more. This collection makes a great gift for the strong woman in your life. It's available from our website at www.spiderroadpess.com and on Amazon.

Up, Do: Flash Fiction by Women Writers

Edited by Patricia Flaherty Pagan

Discover thirty-three intriguing, very short stories. Featuring new flash fiction by award-winningwriter Kathryn Kulpa, best-selling novelist Donna Hill, novelist and poet Catherine Edmunds, science fiction writer Melissa J. Lytton, and many others. The broad range of evocative fiction in this collection makes it a favorite in creative writing workshops. This anthology is available from the Spider Road Press website, in select independent bookstores, and on Amazon.

Eve's Requiem: Tales of Women, Mystery, and Horror

Edited by Patricia Flaherty Pagan and Fern Brady

Enjoy thirteen stories of peril and survival while sipping tea on a dark night. Featuring new horror, dark mystery, and crime stories from celebrated writers such as Pamela Fagan Hutchins, Catherine Edmunds, E.L. Russell, Patricia Flaherty Pagan, and

Pushcart Prize nominee Erika D. Price. This eerie anthology is available from the Spider Road Press website and on Amazon.

5% for healing: Five percent of the proceeds from all Spider Road Press anthologies benefits charities that address the issues of sexual assault, domestic violence & supporting veterans.

www.spiderroadpress.com